Legend
of the
Fire King

by Alicia Ripper

RoseDog Books
PITTSBURGH, PENNSYLVANIA 15238

RoseDog Books
585 Alpha Drive
Pittsburgh, PA 15238
Visit our website at *www.rosedogbookstore.com*

ISBN: 979-8-88729-436-0
eISBN: 979-8-88729-936-5

"Congratulations, My Queen! It's another boy!" The midwife announces happily as she wraps the young boy in a blanket. She hands both babies to the Queen. "Can you believe it?! Twins! My Husband will be thrilled." Queen Alora sighs blissfully. "What will you call them?" Tessie asks warmly. "Hmmm, this young man shall be named Merrick." The Queen states thoughtfully looking adoringly at the baby on the right. "His younger brother will be called Mortimer." The Queen announces sweetly as she smiles at the baby boy on the left. Queen Alora cannot wait until her husband, King Marius, returns home. He will be so surprised to learn he will have two heirs to the throne. She received word late last night that Wallbren surrendered and a treaty is in the works. The King believes it will only be a couple more weeks before he returns.

Just then baby Merrick sneezes and red sparks come out his nose. The sparks land at the foot of the bed and start a fire. "Tessie!!" Queen Alora cries out in a panic. Tessie grabs the pitcher of water sitting on the bedside table and quickly douses the flames. Merrick smiles and coos at the spectacle while Mortimer starts to cry. "Tessie, take Merrick." The Queen commands urgently. The midwife scoops up baby Merrick so the Queen can comfort baby Mortimer. Queen Alora starts to cry. How could this happen?! How could one of her baby's be born cursed?! "What am I going to do?!" The Queen wails as she rocks Mortimer in her arms. Everyone knows her Husband hates magic and mystical creatures. He's never going to accept a son who can create fire. What if he blames her for the child being cursed? What if he hates her for birthing an abomination? What if he locks her up and takes both her sons away from her? She can't have that. She doesn't want to lose her husband or her sons. She looks down at Mortimer whom has fallen asleep. She kisses him, glad she has one normal son. She has a normal son. The Queen realizes the King is only expecting her to have one child and comes up with a plan.

She tells Tessie to take Merrick to the Blacksmith in the woods. Christian the Blacksmith and his wife, Maya are wonderful people. She knows her Husband frowns upon mingling with the commoners and usually she doesn't, but Maya was so bubbly and kind when she first met her three years ago when her horse lost a shoe, the Queen couldn't help but become acquaintances with her and Christian. Christian is the only one she lets touch her horse anymore. Queen Alora knows they will take good care of Merrick, especially since Maya can't have children though she's always wanted them.

"Make sure you are not seen with the child and if anyone asks, tell them I gave birth to one son, Mortimer, understand?" The Queen instructs coolly though she gives Tessie a knowing look and adds a hard edge to her voice when asking for comprehension. Tessie nods. "Yes, your Highness. You only gave birth to one son." She confirms anxiously. "Good. Now I suggest you hide Merrick in the basket of soiled clothes and be gone before he sets anything else on fire." Queen Alora remarks sharply. "Of course, your Highness." Tessie replies quickly with a bow. Tessie sets the sleeping Merrick on the laundry and covers him with one of the shirts. She has her hand on the door handle when the Queen calls out, "Oh and Tessie, tell Christian and

Maya I will build them a grand workshop for taking in the abandoned baby I found down by the stream." Tessie nods before hastily bowing out of the room. Tessie tells the Guard outside that the Queen had a son and to not disturb them because she and the baby are resting. She will send a Maid up in an hour to check on them. Then she quickly strolls down the hall to her chambers.

Tessie sews a hidden pouch into the underside of her dress, tucks baby Merrick inside it, and smuggles him out of the Kingdom. Once she reaches the woods, Tessie removes Merrick from the pouch, removes his blanket and rubs dirt on him to look like he was found lying in the woods. Tessie proceeds to run with the child to the blacksmith's home. She sees the Blacksmith's wife hanging up clothes to dry. Tessie rushes toward her. "Please help me! I need you to take care of this child the Queen found on her walk!" Tessie bursts out breathing heavily as she holds out baby Merrick to her. "What?" Maya asks baffled as she slowly takes the child. Tessie gulps in a couple breaths of air before responding, "The Queen was out for a walk over by the stream with me because she was tired of being cooped up in the Castle. She found this baby sleeping in the grass near the stream. There was no one else around so she figured the child to be abandoned." Tessie rattles off before sucking in more air. "The poor dear." Maya says sympathetically, looking at the sleeping boy. Tessie nods, "Yes, the Queen was horrified that someone could abandon an innocent child. Then she became queasy so she asked me to bring the child to you while her guards escorted her back to the castle." Tessie pants, still trying to catch her breath, holding her side. "Really?" Maya asks hopefully as she strokes the boy's cheek with her index finger, smiling at the beautiful boy. Tessie nods. "The Queen remembered how much you wanted a child so she knows you will take good care of him. She said she will even build you a Grand workshop and home to raise the child in."

she assures Maya. Maya looks up at Tessie in surprise. "Oh, she doesn't need to do that. I would be honored to raise this child as my own. My home is sufficient enough." Maya states happily as she admires the beautiful baby in her arms. Tessie shrugs. "I know, but the Queen wants to. She only requests that you call him Merrick because that's the name that came to her when she first saw the child." Tessie informs Maya rapidly. "Merrick. It does suit him." Maya says dreamily. "Great. Well, I must return to the Queen. I bid you good day." Tessie blurts out hastily then takes off running. Maya looks up in surprise at how fast the lady left, and then smiles as she looks down at baby Merrick. "Let's go inside so you can meet your new Daddy." Maya whispers excitedly to a sleeping Merrick.

Christian is delighted by the sight of a son and the idea of a new home. That evening they find out about Merrick's gift. Maya is startled at first, but then just laughs; excited her baby is magical. Christian just shakes his head in amusement. "Well at least were used to working around fire." He jokes as he kisses his wife on the cheek.

True to the Queen's word, two days after the announcement of her giving birth to a son; workers appear in Christian and Maya's neck of the woods. They start constructing their new home and shop twenty yards back from their current home. Christian helps with the layout and after eight weeks; their home is complete. Though it looks more like a fort than a home, Maya doesn't mind. She thinks it is beautiful. There are 22foot high stone walls in a rectangle shape. The house and shop are at one end and the rest is an open courtyard. The entrance has two heavy 10foot tall wooden doors; a perfect place to raise their son. Maya suspects the boy had been awake when the Queen found him and she saw his powers and she wanted to keep the boy safe. Though, there isn't too much worry of that; most people don't venture out into the woods. Usually her husband just loads up their wagon once a week with wares he's made and takes them to the Castle to sell.

Merrick is five, when Maya finds out the truth from Christian. The Queen's son, Mortimer is the spitting image of Merrick, except the King's heir has blonde hair and brown eyes and Merrick has Dark brown hair, almost black, and gold eyes. The Queen hadn't found Merrick; she'd given birth to Merrick. That explains why she always looks so forlorn when she sees Merrick. Maya understands why the Queen gave up Merrick for fear of her Husband's reaction, but why lie to them about it? They'll keep her secret; for, neither one want to lose Merrick. Maya loves her son and would never do anything to jeopardize his safety. Though Christian did point out they are going to have to come up with a reason to tell Merrick why he needs to keep his face hidden. That night Maya comes up with an idea.

The following morning, Maya sends her husband back into town to buy her some fabric. When he returns, Maya spends the day sewing while Christian keeps an eye on Merrick and ensures Merrick stays out of sight when a customer comes calling. That evening after Merrick finishes his dinner, Maya sits him down in the living room and presents him with his brand new cloak.

"What is it?" young Merrick asks curiously as he holds up the odd piece of apparel. His Mom smiles. "It's a cloak. I'll need you to wear this from now on and you'll need to make sure you wear the hood up whenever you go outside or we have a visitor over." Maya explains gently as she helps him put it on. She's glad to see she made the hood deep enough that it completely hides his face. "Why?" Merrick asks in confusion as he pushes the hood down. Maya smiles sadly at her son. "To hide your face" she replies. "Why?" Merrick asks still confused. Maya takes a deep breath, "You have to hide your face from the outside world because it is a reminder of dark and troubled times. If people see your face they will fear and resent you. They may even try to hurt you out of anger." His Mom sighs warily. "I have a bad face?" Little Merrick asks stunned and saddened by the news. "Yes." Maya states regrettably. She sees how upset her son is about the news and it breaks her heart. She kneels down and pulls him into a hug. "But, YOU also have a good heart and that's what we want people to see; not the bad memories your face stirs, but the kindness of your heart that evokes happiness in others. They will see nothing but how wonderful you are as long as you keep your face hidden, okay?" His Mom assures him lovingly. Merrick nods in understanding. "So, you promise to keep your face hidden when you're outside and whenever we have guests over?" Maya asks for assurance as she leans back to look her son in the eyes. "I promise." Merrick agrees in a disheartened tone. His Mother gives him another hug and a kiss on the cheek before standing up. She turns to walk back into the kitchen when Merrick asks woefully looking at his feet, "Mommy, does my face bother you or Daddy?" "Oh baby, of course not. We love everything about you and that will never change." She assures him earnestly walking back over to him, kneeling down, and cupping his chin to tilt his head up so he is looking at her. Merrick sees the sincerity in her face and smiles at her. Maya smiles back and gives him another hug. Merrick pulls the hood back up and ventures outside.

Merrick did his best to keep his promise to his Mother. Though being a young boy, who is more focused on seeking adventure and having fun, Merrick often forgot to pull his hood up. His Mother had to constantly remind him. After a few close calls with customers seeing him, Merrick's Dad makes him wear the hood up all the time unless given permission to lower it.

A few months later, Maya takes Merrick for a walk in the woods to a nearby meadow where they have a picnic. During lunch, Maya sees the sky darken and the wind starts to pick up. Maya tells Merrick he'll have to finish his sandwich on the way back. She starts putting things away when they hear a crack of thunder.

"Merrick, stay close. I'm just about ready…" Maya directs her son hastily as she finishes folding up the blanket and stuffs it in her basket. Her voice trails off as she glances behind her and sees Merrick isn't there. She turns around to see Merrick fifty yards away, running towards the opposite tree line where smoke is coming out above the trees. "MERRICK!" Maya screams but the wind must carry her voice away because he doesn't turnaround to look at her. He just keeps running towards the wrong trees and the smoke. Maya runs after her son screaming for him to stop. She panics and drops her picnic basket when she sees Merrick disappear into the trees. The wind is really howling and it starts to pour as Maya sprints after her son. Maya reaches the trees but there is no sign of Merrick. She has to slow her pace so she doesn't trip. The good thing was the farther into the woods she went the quieter the wind got. Maya is about to call out her son's name when she spots him thirty yards in front of her standing in front of a huge fire. "Merrick." She utters in horror as she stumbles forward. Her horror turns to shock as she realizes the fire is reducing in size. She walks slowly towards her son hypnotized by the shrinking flames. By the time she reaches Merrick, the fire is gone. Maya looks down at her son in astonishment. She knows he has the ability to create fire. He is always performing for her with these little dancing flames he would create, but she had no idea he could extinguish a massive fire. Too stunned to speak, she stays silent as she watches Merrick walk over to a nearby bundle of brush that the fire had not touched and scoop up a small wolf cub that had gotten tangled up in the brush.

Though his hood hides his face, Merrick turns and grins at his Mom, proud of his accomplishment, having no idea he'd scared his

Mom by running off. "Can I keep him?" He asks hopefully. Maya drops to her knees and pulls Merrick and the squirming pup into a tight embrace. "I was so scared. I thought I was going to lose you." His Mom whispers, tears of relief streaming down her cheeks as it continues to rain down on them. "I'm sorry Mommy. I didn't mean to scare you. I just wanted to see what was causing the smoke and when I got here, I saw Wolf stuck in the pile of sticks with the fire headed straight for him. I had to stop it. Please don't be mad." Merrick apologizes contritely becoming more upset as he kept talking until his own tears started to fall as he pleads with his Mom not to be angry with him. Maya lets him go and gently pushes him back as she fervently shakes her head. She pushes his hood down so she can see his face and strokes his cheeks. "I'm not mad." She states brushing her tears away and smiling at him. She reaches back out to gently wipe his tears away. "I'm not mad. I was just scared you were going to get hurt, but you didn't. You're fine and what you did was simply amazing." She explains happily through her tears. "So can I keep Wolf?" He asks uncertainly holding the wolf cub out so she can see him. "Wolf?" Maya sniffs amused by her son's name for the little black pup. "Wouldn't you rather call him Soot?" She asks teasingly. Merrick's face lights up. "So, I can keep him?" he asks excitedly. His Mom nods and Merrick throws his arms around her though he is careful not to hurt Wolf. "Thank you, Mommy. You can call him Soot if you like, but I like Wolf." He states happily letting go of his Mom. Maya smiles then blows out a breath. "Just promise me, next time you'll take me along with you instead of running off by yourself." She requests still slightly frazzled. Merrick nods as he pulls his hood back up. Maya smiles, glad her son finally remembered to pull his hood up without being reminded. He holds out his free hand and they walk back to the meadow. When they arrive at the edge of the woods, the wind has died but it continues to rain. They retrieve the picnic basket and walk home in the rain.

When they arrive home, Merrick relays their adventure to his father, while his Mother makes a bed for Soot/Wolf in a corner of the Kitchen. Merrick hopes he and Wolf will be best friends, but he discovers quickly that Wolf likes his Mom and prefers to hang out with her. The wolf pup follows Maya around wherever she goes and only hangs out with Merrick when Maya tells him to. The pup also refuses to answer to Wolf and will only answer to the name Soot, so Merrick begrudgingly starts calling the young pup Soot.

15 years later

"Remember Queen Isabo, King Marius despises magic so please try to contain your powers." Kelsie reminds the Queen, who has the power to create and manipulate snow and ice, as she helps the Queen prepare to dock. "I know Kelsie. I will conceal my powers. I know how important this deal is to the Kingdom and I won't let the King's narrow minded views bother me. We will stay on subject, only discuss the trade of coal for wool and everything will be fine ... right?" The Queen recites confidently until the end as anxiety kicks in. "Absolutely, it will be a piece of cake." Kelsie, her advisor, assures her brightly as she helps Queen Isabo with her coat.

"Unbelievable." Prince Mortimer mutters irritably. He just finished reading his Mother's journal and found out he has an identical twin brother named Merrick who lives with the Blacksmith out in the woods. No wonder she always insists on going there to get her horse shoed. She goes to see HIM. Mortimer wants to question her about it, but he needs to get ready for Queen Isabo of Arenia's arrival.

Rumor is she's some kind of freak that can manipulate ice. Personally, he doesn't see why they need to trade with her kingdom. They've done fine in the past without having to deal with them. Why start now? Mortimer sighs moodily as he puts his Mother's journal back and sneaks out of his parent's bedroom.

Queen Isabo takes a deep breath and slowly lets it out for courage as her footman opens the door to her carriage. He helps her out and she lays eyes on the castle for the first time. It seems cold and uninviting, but Isabo holds her head high as she walks towards the doorman who seems nervous. "Queen Isabo of Arenia, Welcome to Octavian. King Marius and the royal family await you in the great hall, so if you would please follow me." The man announces obediently as he bows to her. "Of Course." Isabo replies indifferently. Queen Isabo follows the portly man into the castle down a corridor into a glorious Great hall. At the far end sits the King, Queen and the Prince. They rise as Queen Isabo enters the room. Isabo is surprised at how tall King Marius is. He's at least 6'3 with short Dark brown hair almost black and steely brown eyes where his wife is about her height at 5'9 but has golden blonde hair with eyes to match. Then there is the Prince; a spitting image of his father except a couple inches shorter and blonde hair like his mother.

"My Majesties, May I present Queen Isabo of Arenia." The man announces her then quickly takes his leave. "Queen Isabo? I must say, you are quite a bit younger than I was expecting." King Marius states calculatingly as he stares at the young white haired beauty with pale lavender eyes while he walks down to greet her. "Is that a problem" Queen Isabo asks speculatively. "Not at all; in fact, it's a nice change of pace." King Marius says sweetly as he kisses her knuckles. "You are enchanting." Queen Alora states warmly as she inclines her head in greeting to Isabo. "As are you, Queen Alora." Isabo replies politely bowing back to her. "Dear, why don't you show Queen Isabo to the Dining hall while I have a quick word with our son?" King Marius suggests sweetly to his wife. "Of course." Queen Alora replies awkwardly giving her husband a curious look, wondering what he's up to. "Excellent, we will just be a few moments and then we'll join you and talk trade while we dine." The King states jovially. Isabo nods in agreement and follows Queen Alora out a side door.

King Marius waits until the women are out of sight then turns to his son. "I want you to woo Queen Isabo." King Marius states firmly. "What?!" Mortimer asks in disbelief. "I want you to sweep that girl off her feet and convince her to marry you." The King commands sternly. "But ..." Prince Mortimer sputters, "I don't want to marry her." Mortimer pouts grouchily. "I don't care what you want. A marriage of our two Kingdoms will ensure our survival, especially since we are on the brink of another war with Wallbren." The King snaps and then narrows his gaze at his son. "You ARE going to charm Queen Isabo and be at her beck and call during her stay. You WILL win her over or I will find someone else to succeed my rule of Octavian." King Marius threatens his son. Mortimer's eyes widen in fear and just as quickly narrow in anger. "I don't believe you. You'd never let someone not of your blood rule this place." Mortimer remarks haughtily. "Then I guess I'll just give it to your brother." King Marius growls. The King smirks when he sees the shocked look on his son's face. "Yes, I know all about your twin so unless you want to switch places with him; you will do what I say." The King advises coldly. "Fine, I'll make Isabo fall in love with me." Mortimer agrees in disgruntlement. "Good, now let's go join the women." His father says coolly; happy his son made the right decision.

They join the women and the King asks if Queen Isabo would mind holding off talking trade until after they eat. "I don't like to do business on an empty stomach." The King explains cordially. Isabo smiles politely. "I don't mind at all." She replies kindly. They share some small talk and Queen Isabo describes Arenia to them. "You know, since this is your first visit here, maybe we should wait on this business transaction until tomorrow evening." Prince Mortimer suggests thoughtfully. Queen Isabo raises her eyebrows in curious surprise. "I was just thinking, I could take you on a tour of the Kingdom tomorrow and you could see if there is anything else you might like to negotiate for besides our abundance of coal." Mortimer proposes innocently with a friendly smile. "I think that's a great idea son." King Marius beams happily. "What say you?" The King asks Queen Isabo excitedly. Isabo swallows nervously, completely taken aback by this turn of events. "Don't you think that's a bit unfair? As I will have seen all you have to offer, but you won't be able to see My Kingdom with all its wares." She asks hesitantly. The King shakes his head. "Not at all. I trust if you find anything else that interests you, you will offer a fair trade of something of equal value to me." The King states merrily. "Alright then, I would be honored to tour your Kingdom with Prince Mortimer." Queen Isabo says calmly though her heart's pounding; not sure this is a good idea. She smiles warmly at Prince Mortimer as the King makes a couple of suggestions of where they should go. "Oh Mort, you have to take her to my blacksmith." Queen Alora chimes in happily squeezing her son's hand. She turns to Isabo, "He makes the most beautiful sculptures with metal. The candelabra, you were admiring earlier, is one of his pieces." Queen Alora explains brightly to Isabo. "Oh, I don't …" the King starts to say dismissively when Mortimer cuts him off, "That's a great idea Mother!" He exclaims excitedly as an idea forms of how he can get rid of all his problems. "I'll make that our last stop." Prince Mortimer beams. "Sound good." Queen Isabo says lightly though she finds the

Prince's behavior unsettling. He seemed a little too enthusiastic to her considering when she first saw him he looked at her with disdain and didn't even greet her. More than likely his Father is making him be nice to her, so tomorrow should be interesting. After dinner is over with, Prince Mortimer escorts Queen Isabo to the room she will be staying in. He wishes her goodnight with a kiss on her hand then strolls down the hall to his chambers.

Mortimer waits until he's safely in his room with the door shut before he shivers and wipes his mouth off. Her hand was ice cold. What a freak. No one said anything but he saw her hands glow white and white sparks emit from her hands causing her utensils and goblet to develop a thin sheet of ice. He can't wait until tomorrow. He'll be the polite charming guy while he's with her. They will tour the Kingdom and then go to the woods. He will take her horseback riding deep into the forest and spook her horse, so it runs away. He'll come back to the Castle and say she has been kidnapped by his brother. With any luck she'll be killed by wolves. His brother will be blamed for her death and hung for his crimes and then Mortimer will no longer have to marry the 'Ice Queen' and there will no longer be anyone to contest his rightful place as future King. Prince Mortimer smiles evilly at his brilliant plan as he turns in for the night.

The following day, Prince Mortimer and Queen Isabo are walking around the town Market accompanied by four guards when the Prince spots a Gypsy selling herbal medicines. The Queen is busy looking at silk scarves so Mortimer excuses himself and wanders over to the Gypsy's cart. He returns to the Queen's side ten minutes later pleased at his good fortune. "Queen Isabo, how would you feel about joining me for a picnic?" Mortimer asks excitedly. "That sounds lovely." Isabo responds happily as she pays for the periwinkle scarf she found. Queen Isabo is surprised at how much she is enjoying herself and the Prince's company. He's been nothing but a complete gentleman and his good mood has put her in a delightful mood. The Prince escorts her around to the different venues and shops. He lets her pick out the food for their picnic and he selects the wine. They ride in the Royal coach to the edge of the woods where Prince Mortimer suggests they shed their security and pretend to be normal folk out for a ride. Isabo is not to keen on the idea. "Aw come on, where's your sense of adventure?" Prince Mortimer Urges good-naturedly. He still sees her hesitancy. "Please, I promise you won't regret it." He coaxes charmingly. Queen Isabo laughs at his boyish charm and nods. "Alright." She agrees and dismisses her two guards. Prince Mortimer has his guards unhitch two of the horses and load their picnic onto the back of his horse, and then he orders them to take the coach back to the castle. The Prince takes Queen Isabo to see the Blacksmith first. Luckily, his brother is not there, so they stay awhile so Queen Isabo can see the different pieces the Blacksmith and his son have made while she visits with him. The Blacksmith gives her a silver snowflake pendant that his son had made. Queen Isabo thanks the Blacksmith for his kind gift and ties the twine chain around her wrist and wears the pendant as a bracelet. The Queen and the Prince leave there and ride deeper into the woods until they find a beautiful meadow to stop and have their picnic.

Prince Mortimer sets everything up as Queen Isabo looks around. She pays no attention to the Prince so she doesn't see him take out a small vile, the one he had bought from the Gypsy woman and hid in his inner breast pocket, and pour the contents into Isabo's drink. He calls for her to come join him after the liquid dissolves into the wine. Queen Isabo takes a seat on the blanket and the Prince hands her a goblet. "Let's make a toast." Prince Mortimer suggests merrily. "What shall we toast to?" Queen Isabo asks amusedly. The Prince thinks a moment then raises his glass, "How about, here's to spending a great day with great company and hoping this isn't the last." He toasts happily giving Queen Isabo a smoldering look. Isabo blushes as she clinks her goblet with his and takes a long drink.

Isabo doesn't know what to say. She likes Prince Mortimer, he is definitely a lot nicer than she expected. He's also handsome, but there's just something about him that unsettles her. He seems almost too nice, like he's trying too hard. She isn't sure, but she needs him to know she only wants to be his friend. "Prince Mor—-"Queen Isabo starts to say then passes out.

Prince Mortimer smiles wickedly at the sleeping Queen. The Gypsy hadn't been lying when she said the sleeping draft worked quickly. The Prince picks up the sleeping Queen and un-ceremonially shoves her back up on the horse. Then he points the horse towards the dark woods and smacks the horse's rump; which, sends the horse running into wildlife infested country. "I hope you get eaten by a bear." He mutters darkly as he sits back down on the blanket and enjoys his private feast. He waits until sunset before he packs up, finds a jagged rock, cuts his cheek and ruffles up his hair and clothes. He Mounts his horse and runs out of the meadow toward the Kingdom and hollers for help when he finally reaches the edge of the forest.

Queen Isabo comes awake to find herself dangling half way off a horse. She slides down to the ground. She sees the horse has his reins tangled up in some branches and that it is night time. Fortunately, the moon is bright enough that she can make out her immediate surroundings even with the heavy tree cover. She untangles the reins, climbs back up on the horse and leads him forward hoping she is going towards the castle. She rides through the woods trying to figure out what happened. The only conclusion she could come up with is the Prince drugged her, but why? What good could possibly come of stranding her out in the middle of nowhere? She won't freeze to death. She's immune to the cold since her gift is wielding the snow and ice. Is he hoping she gets eaten by a bear? The Queen doesn't know. She is still groggy from whatever the Prince drugged her with and can't think clearly. She sighs warily. Well, whatever his plan was, it is going to fail. She will find her way back and when she does that cretin and his father are going to get an ear full.

Queen Isabo doesn't know how long she's been wandering through the woods when she sees a fire in a distant clearing. She gently squeezes the horse's flanks and sends him trotting towards the fire. When she arrives at what looks like a campsite, there is no one around.

"Hello? Is anyone out there?" She calls out to the nearby trees as she dismounts her horse. She hears a twig snap. Queen Isabo looks to her left and then her right. She gasps when she sees a big black wolf step out of the shadows twenty feet in front of her. Queen Isabo takes a step back, calls upon her powers making her hands glow, and throws out her hands sending white sparks towards the wolf. The sparks land around the wolf turning to ice and grows all around into an icy cage in which the wolf cannot escape.

"Whoa, How did you do that?" a male voice asks curiously. The Queen looks around frantically, but sees no one. "Who's there?" she asks fearfully as her eyes dart about while her heart feels like it's going to pop out of her chest; its pounding so hard. "A friend of the wolf." The male voice says amusedly. She looks at the wolf with wide eyes and sees it is studying her with interest, but it is not growling at her. The wolf doesn't seem to want to attack her. Queen Isabo calms down as she looks around again. She still doesn't see anyone. Where is this guy? "Show yourself." She demands becoming annoyed talking to air. "Promise you won't encage me and I'll come down." The voice negotiates playfully. Tired and cranky, Isabo sighs in frustration. "Fine, I won't cage you. Now, will you please present yourself?" She asks impatiently. "Alright, alright, don't have a meltdown." The male voice laughs. Queen Isabo sees movement in one of the trees just as a man swings down from a large branch and drops to his feet. He straightens up and Isabo judges he is the same height and physique as Prince Mortimer though this guy has a deeper voice. He is wearing a cloak with his hood up so she can't see his face. The man walks over to the caged wolf and pokes the cage. "Impressive." He remarks admiringly as he circles the cage.

"What do you think, Soot?" He asks kneeling down in front of the wolf. The wolf growls at him. "Hey, don't blame me. Ice lady is the one who put you in here." He remarks defensively to the wolf. The wolf appears to glare at him as he growls again. "Hey, cut the attitude or I'll leave you in there." The man warns the wolf teasingly. "Promise not to move until the lady says you can and I'll remove the front for you." He bargains with the wolf in a serious tone. Isabo watches as the wolf appears to huff at the gentleman, but then lies down. Her jaw drops as she sees the man magically melt the four bars in front of the wolf. Even more surprising is the wolf doesn't move.

"See, he won't ..." The mystery guy starts to say good naturedly as he stands up until she strikes him in the shoulder with a snowball. "Hey, what was that for?" he questions sourly; offended more than anything. "That was for scaring me and this is for ignoring me after the fact." She snaps irritably as she throws another snowball at him. He blocks it from hitting his chest with his forearm. "Well then you shouldn't wake a guy out of a dead sleep if you want hospitality." He retorts condescendingly. "Hey, Stop that!" He yelps as she chucks another snowball at his head. The man dodges it just in time. He takes a step towards her. "Well, if I had KNOWN you were sleeping, I wouldn't have woken you." She replies haughtily, taking a step closer to him. "Considering its night time it would have been a good assumption." He grumbles in a dry, surly tone. She throws another snowball at him and he counters with a fireball. The two balls strike each other and vaporize. Then Queen Isabo sees the man fall to the ground as the wolf pounces on his back and sits on top of him. Isabo smiles at the sight. The guy grunts. "Get off, Soot. It wasn't going to hit her." He grumbles in annoyance. Soot doesn't move. Isabo giggles, "I like your wolf." She calls Soot over to her. Soot jumps off the guy and trots over to Isabo. She kneels down and pets the wolf. "Traitor" The man mutters sourly as he rises to his knees. Queen Isabo notices he is clutching his hood as he stands up as if he is afraid to let it fall back so she can see his face. *How weird?* Queen Isabo thinks before narrowing her gaze. "Well, maybe he likes people with good manners." She remarks insinuatingly. Mystery guy glares at her. "Fine. You keep him" he huffs sulkily. He snaps his fingers, extinguishing the fire and spins on his heel. The hooded man takes a couple steps towards the trees when Soot whines at him.

"What's wrong boy?" Queen Isabo asks with concern as she scratches his neck. "He's afraid of the dark." The man sighs warily, then throws out a red spark from his hand and the fire blazes a new. Queen Isabo watches in stunned silence as the guy walks back over to the tree he came from and climbs back up. She looks at the wolf and smiles. "I see why you hang out with him." She whispers to Soot warmly and gives him a hug.

Isabo yawns as she lets go of the wolf and stands up. She eyes the area and then uses her powers to erect an ice fort around the fire with walls that stretch 15 feet high. She wraps her cloak around herself like a blanket and lies down. Soot curls up beside her and they drift off to sleep.

Merrick sits up in the tree marveling at her ice fortress. He can't believe he actually met someone who has powers like him. He often wonders what it would be like to have a friend; especially one with powers, someone who would understand the challenges of living with a gift. Someone he could confess all his fears and worries to without being judged knowing they shared similar or even the same fears and obstacles. Maybe this girl is what he has been searching for. He sighs dreamily as he looks up to the sky and makes a wish that the ice maiden will be his friend.

The following morning, Merrick climbs down out of the tree and circles the ice box. He discovers Mystery girl didn't build in a door. Merrick hears Soot whining, so he uses his powers to burn an entryway. He barely dodges Soot as the wolf comes charging out through the door. Merrick steps inside and sees the girl still fast asleep. She is beautiful with her long white hair and spunky attitude. She looks to be about his age though she is about six inches shorter than him. He smiles at how peaceful she looks and instantly feels guilty for his behavior last night. Not wanting to scare her, Merrick exits the fort and decides to go scrounge up some breakfast.

Queen Isabo wakes up to the smell of something delicious. She sits up and stretches. She sees the fire has gone out and so has Soot. Then she notices the 'door' in the wall. Hooded guy must have created it to let Soot out. Queen Isabo stands up and uses her powers to turn the ice walls to snow that scatters over the ground. "Whoa!" she hears the mystery guy blurt out in awe. She turns to where she hears his voice and sees him sitting on a log a few feet away holding a frying pan in his right hand while tossing food to Soot with his left hand. "Morning." He greets her cheerfully as she walks over and sits down on a log opposite of his. "Good Morning." She replies blearily before stifling another yawn glad to see he seems to be in a better mood than last night. "Would you like some breakfast?" he asks pleasantly. "Yes, please. I'm famished." She replies good-naturedly, relieved he is nice enough to share. He grabs a plate and fork from his satchel then slides the meat and eggs on to the plate. He stands up, walks over to her and hands her the plate and utensil. "Thank you." Queen Isabo states appreciatively. She takes a bite of eggs when she notices his is still standing in front of her.

She swallows and then asks uncertainly, "Is something wrong?" He points to her wrist, "Where did you get that?" he asks inquisitively. She looks down at her wrist and sees the snowflake pendant as the object he is referring to. She smiles as she recalls the nice man who gave it to her. "The Blacksmith I visited yesterday gave it to me." Queen Isabo explains reminiscently. "You met my Dad?" He asks in surprise. "Your father is the Queen's Blacksmith?" she counters in an equally surprised voice. The man nods solemnly. "Do you want it back?" Isabo asks uncertainly confused to why he seems so sad about it. He shakes his head as he backs away from her. "No. You may keep it. It suits you." He replies serenely. "You sure? You seem kind of attached to it." Queen Isabo inquires speculatively. Mystery guy sits back down before he replies lightly, "I'm sure. It was a gift I made for my Mother. She never wore it because it was so beautiful to her, she was afraid she'd lose it. I'm glad he gave it to you. It's nice to see someone wearing it and it looks good on you." Queen Isabo wishes she could see his face to know if he's being sincere or not, but it remains hidden in the depths of his hood.

They sit in silence for a few minutes while she eats, and he shifts nervously in his seat. "I'm sorry about last night. I shouldn't have been so callous." Merrick blurts out awkwardly; glad she can't see his face as he feels his cheeks redden. Queen Isabo smiles, "It's okay. I shouldn't have thrown snowballs at you." She admits guiltily. He sees the sincerity in her pale lavender eyes and grins. "No worries. You can make it up to me." Merrick states mischievously. "How?"

she asks suspiciously surprised and somewhat impressed by his gall. "Fill these with ice." He requests playfully as he holds out a canteen and a cup to her. Queen Isabo laughs as she fulfills his request. Her eyes widen in fascination as she watches his hands glow red and the ice in the cup melt. He places the cup, now filled with water, down beside her then returns to his seat where he takes a swig from the canteen. "Thank you." Merrick says gratefully as he pours some water into a bowl for Soot.

"Is there anything I can do for you?" Merrick asks whimsically as he stores the canteen back in his bag. Queen Isabo swallows the last of her breakfast, "Would you tell me your name?" She asks hopefully. "It's Merrick." He answers with chagrin, blushing again. "Nice to meet you Merrick. My name is Isabo." She replies brightly. "Is there anything else you need?" Merrick asks amusedly. "I could use an escort back to the Castle." Queen Isabo comments thoughtfully as she looks up at the sky. "I can do that." Merrick replies grinningly.

Isabo watches Merrick as he cleans up their dishes and talks to him about her gift and her home at Arenia and what it was like to grow up there. Merrick tells her about his childhood and how he rescued Soot but, Soot was his Mom's companion up until the day she died. He doesn't mention why he keeps his face hidden, which is what she really wants to know. She asks him about how he learned to control his powers hoping that would lead him to tell her about his reason for hiding his face. It doesn't. Like her, he didn't have trouble controlling his powers because his parents had been so supportive and caring it had been easy to master his gift. Isabo does confess to him that she has trouble controlling the force of her power when she is angry. They talk about their likes and interests, yet her curiosity of his hood gets the better of her so she finally asks, "Why won't you let me see your face?"

Merrick stops drying the frying pan to look toward her. He had been avoiding the topic in hopes she wouldn't ask. He has been enjoying their conversation and she seems to be enjoying it as well and he doesn't want to ruin that by bringing up his hideousness. They are just starting to become friends and he would hate to lose this friendship over his appearance. He really likes Isabo and fears if she sees his face, she will run away screaming. He figures the least he can do is tell her the truth and hope she doesn't push the subject. He shrugs his shoulders. "My face is offensive and I don't want to scare you." He states simply as he goes back to drying his dishes. Queen Isabo could have sworn she heard a hint of sadness in his voice as if he's shown someone his face before and they reacted badly to it. She figures he must have horrific scars from some accident he had while experimenting with his powers. "I don't scare easily." Isabo coaxes warmly hoping he'll push the hood back. He shakes his head as he puts the last of his dishes away. "I can't risk it. It would be very difficult to guide you …" Merrick explains regrettably then stops when he hears Soot growl.

He looks over at the wolf and sees Soot is staring into the woods behind him. Merrick motions Isabo to stay quiet and to not move as he stealthily disappears into the woods. Queen Isabo waits anxiously for Merrick's return. It feels like an eternity passes before he comes running out of the woods. She opens her mouth to ask what it is but he shakes his head at her and snatches his satchel from the ground. Isabo stands up as he motions her over to the horse.

"There's an army headed this way. We need to get out of here. We need to warn the Kingdom." Merrick states in a low urgent voice. Isabo nods in understanding her eyes fearful. Merrick assists her in mounting the horse then climbs up behind her. "Soot!" He hollers in a hushed tone as he grabs the reins. "Wow, you're really warm." Isabo murmurs unexpectedly; surprised by the heat rolling off Merrick. "Yeah, sorry. I tend to run a few degrees warmer than most." He whispers distractedly as he waits for Soot to jog over to them. "Follow us." He orders the wolf quietly then spurs the horse and they take off running.

As they near the Kingdom of Octavian, Merrick wonders if he should stop at the edge of the woods and let Isabo warn the Kingdom by herself. He's not allowed to go into the Kingdom. Due to his gift and face, his parents thought it best he stay away from Octavian. He had made a deal with them: He can travel where ever he likes as long as he never sets foot in Octavian. Merrick has kept that promise for fifteen years, but surely his Dad would be okay with him breaking the rule just this once in order to protect the Kingdom? Merrick realizes he won't have to break his promise when he sees Octavian Guards a mile ahead. He can tell them and they can relay the information to the King.

Merrick pulls the horse up short as they reach the guards. "Sirs, there is an ..." Merrick starts to warn them when the guard in front of him shouts, "Grab Him!" Two sets of arms reach up and pull him off the horse. "What are you doing?!" Queen Isabo snaps incredulously as one of the guards slaps irons on Merrick's wrists. "We're arresting this criminal for kidnapping you Queen Isabo." The guard near her states firmly. "Queen!" Merrick utters in shock. "He didn't kidnap me." Queen Isabo retorts angrily as she sees Merrick give a slight shake of his head to call off Soot. "It doesn't matter. We have it on good authority this imposter is planning an attack on the Prince." One of the guards holding Merrick informs the Queen Haughtily. "What?!" Merrick blurts out in disbelief. "That's a Lie!" Merrick barks angrily. "Shut up rat." The second guard snarls and elbows Merrick in the stomach. "Stop It! Leave him alone!" Isabo shrieks. "I'm sorry, your Majesty, but this impersonator must pay for his crimes." The guard near her remarks coldly. "What crimes, I haven't done anything. I don't … NO! Don't!!" Merrick spouts angrily and confused by what was happening, and then shouts for the guard to stop as he grabs a hold of Merrick's hood. The guard ignores Merrick's cry and yanks the hood down.

Queen Isabo gasps as she sees a shoulder length brown haired, golden eyed version of Prince Mortimer. Merrick quickly turns his face and closes his eyes. "I'm sorry. I know it's bad, but you've got to believe me. I don't want to hurt anyone. I've never even met the Prince. I don't even know what he looks like!" Merrick pleads aloud to Isabo desperately. The guards drag him towards the Kingdom as he continues to plead his innocence. Queen Isabo watches in stunned silence as they drag Merrick away; too shocked to say or do anything. She finally snaps out of her stupor when she hears Merrick yell from a distance to look after Soot. Queen Isabo looks over her shoulder and sees Soot pacing in-between two trees about 20 yards away. "Soot, Go home." She commands and watches Soot run off towards the Blacksmith's. Then Isabo turns her attention to the baffled looking guard that stayed with her. "Take me to the King, Now." She orders icily as her reins develop ice on them. She looks down and sees her hands are glowing white. Queen Isabo takes a few deep calming breaths to keep her powers in check so she doesn't hurt the horse. She knows exactly who is behind this charade. Merrick is innocent. She sees her hands turn to normal color. Only one person deserves her wrath and HE is going to rue the day he tried to kill her.

As soon as she reaches the entrance to the Castle, Queen Isabo hops off the horse and lets her fury flourish. Her hands turn a blinding white as white sparks come pouring out of her. The ground turns to ice and the white sparks flow up the walls instantly covering them with a sheet of ice. Queen Isabo storms into the castle with white sparks flurrying around her causing everything in her path to be covered in ice or frozen solid. In fact; the only thing that is still moving are the servants and they are quick to avoid her. She hears the King's laughter coming from the dining hall. Queen Isabo marches to the Entryway and blows the doors open with her powers.

"Have a nice life." The guard says snidely as he finishes chaining Merrick to a wall in his cell of the dungeon. Then he walks away slamming the cell door behind him. Merrick hangs his head in sorrow allowing his hair to hide his face. He still doesn't understand why they are accusing him of impersonating the Prince. He's never seen or heard the Prince so he couldn't pretend he was Prince Mortimer. His Father only told him good things, about the Prince and what a great King he will make, so why would he try and hurt the Prince? Besides, He'd only been trying to help Isabo. Correction, Queen Isabo. She is a Queen and way out of his league. He just hopes she looks after Soot or at least returns him to his father. His father … Hopefully, she'll tell his Dad what happened so he doesn't worry. Maybe …

"Hey, Do I know you?" A wary male voice asks. Without thinking Merrick looks up to see who spoke. He finds a thin worn down man about his father's age with red hair mixed with tufts of grey and curious brown eyes chained to the wall opposite him staring at him in surprise. "Your Majesty, what are you doing in here?" The man breaths in disbelief. Merrick gives him a queer look, "I'm not royalty. I'm a blacksmith." He replies in annoyance while wondering what this guy's problem is. The man gasps in astonishment, "You're the other son!" "What?!" Merrick asks completely baffled by what the man is muttering about. "Do you really have the ability to create and control fire?" The man asks excitedly ignoring Merrick's question. Merrick says nothing; instead, he creates a fire ball in his hand then extinguishes it. "How extraordinary! That must mean the legend is true and the King ..." the man babbles excitedly in a hushed voice before Merrick interrupts him.

"What are you talking about? What Legend?" Merrick questions irritably. The man looks at him is surprise. "You haven't heard the legend of the fire King?" the man asks in shock. "No Mr. Babble I haven't. Would you mind telling me?" Merrick answers in a surly tone. "I would appreciate it if you'd mind your tone, young Prince and my name is Anton, not Mr. Babble." Anton states indignantly. "Fine, but I'm not a Prince. My name is Merrick and I'm the son of Christian the Blacksmith." Merrick replies irritably. Anton looks at him sympathetically. "Poor kid, you don't have a clue who you are." He sighs warily, shaking his head. "I know exactly who I am and I'd appreciate it if you'd either tell me the legend or shut up all together. I don't care which." Merrick growls in an annoyed, defensive voice as he leans his head back and stares at the ceiling. "Alright, I'll tell you the story. No reason to get snippy." Anton replies testily. He clears his throat and in a solemn voice says:

"A long time ago a mighty King named Tyberius ruled this land. He was a fair and gentle King whom the people of Octavian admired and respected. King Tyberius believed with hard work and an open mind anything was possible. His common sense, calm disposition and willingness to listen to the people kept peace across the Land. Though he was gentle he was also feared due to his gift of fire.

The King could create and manipulate the flame. King Tyberius despised violence so in time of war, he would create a wall of fire around the Kingdom that went as high as the tallest tower. He would manipulate the flame so the heat drifted toward the enemy roasting them out while keeping the Kingdom cool. The firewall was so powerful anything thrown in the fire turned to ash. Eventually the enemy would tire and wary of the heat and a surrender would be negotiated.

A treaty would be signed and a huge festival would commence to celebrate new found friends and the end of the war.

The King had a younger brother, Marcus, whom was extremely jealous of his brother because of his special power. Marcus had no special gifts and everyone ignored him. King Tyberius was charismatic and fun loving, where Marcus was stodgy and didn't believe a King should be celebrating with lowly commoners. Prince Marcus believed Royalty should mingle with other royalty and upper classmen only. He also believed a King should be revered as untouchable, not a blabbering fool who would shake anyone's hand. Prince Marcus felt the other Kingdoms mocked them for being crass and disorderly.

Two weeks before King Tyberius was set to wed, the King fell ill. Physicians and healers throughout the land came forth to try and save the King, but alas after four days the great King was dead. As King Tyberius had not yet married; hence had no heir to the throne, Prince Marcus was sworn in as the new ruler of Octavian.

The Kingdom changed overnight. The orphans were no longer able to sleep in the ballroom at night. They were thrown out of the castle, along with anyone else who was not a servant or of noble blood. The servants were instructed to address King Marcus as "Your Highness" or "Your Majesty", but never by his first name. If they did, they would be punished. King Marcus buried his brother that morning and by that afternoon had forbidden the mention of his brother's name.

It is said the people of Octavian noticed the air was chillier than usual on the day the buried their beloved King. Most people thought it appropriate as their King of warmth and kindness was replaced by a King who was cold and cruel. Some had believed that King Tyberius was responsible for their warm and balmy summers and mild winters and would be in for dark and desolate times ahead. There are people whom believe in the tale of the great King and hope one day a new fire King will come and restore peace and prosperity to the land." Anton finishes his story on a wistful note.

"So you think I'm this Tyberius guy reincarnated? I can't be. I'm not of royal blood." Merrick reasons in a doubtful tone. Anton's response is to tell him about the rumor of Queen Alora giving birth to twin boys and how she gave the eldest son to her favorite Blacksmith and his wife due to fear of what the King would do if he found out his eldest son had magical powers. Merrick stares at the ground in silence as all this new information swirls with the memories of his past.

"You're saying my parents aren't really my parents and the reason they kept me hidden is because the Prince is my twin brother?" He asks hollowly for confirmation looking up at Anton. Anton nods sadly and then shivers. "Why didn't they just tell me the truth? Merrick asks meekly looking back down at the ground again and then realizes the answer right after the words leave his mouth. "W-woul-ld y-you h-ha-vve s-st-ta-tayed a-a-w-way i-if th-they h-had?" Anton stammers as he shivers uncontrollably. No, he wouldn't have. Merrick shakes his head then looks around as he sees his breath and Anton shivering terribly.

They watch as white sparks climb the walls and streak across the floor leaving a layer of ice in their wake. Merrick looks around his immediate area and observes that his body heat is melting the ice around him, and then he glances over to Anton and sees him turning blue. Merrick quickly produces a dancing flame and has it wander over to Anton. The flame increases in size and instantly warms Anton. "Thank you." He says appreciatively. Merrick creates more dancing flames and sends them to the other cells. As the layer of ice gets thicker, Merrick realizes what, or more to the point, who is causing it. "Isabo." He breathes in awe.

"I want Merrick released now." Queen Isabo demands crisply as she approaches the end of the table where King Marius and Prince Mortimer are sitting, her glowing hands balled up into fists. King Marius jumps in his seat, startled by her presence. "Queen Isabo! It's good to see you've returned in one piece, but I'm afraid I don't know this Merrick you speak of." The King replies in a bored tone. He frowns at the sight of her glowing fists and the white sparks flowing from that are turning his dining hall into an icy cavern. "Merrick is your son. I know that because he looks just like HIM." Queen Isabo seethes icily pointing at Prince Mortimer who quickly ducks as an icicle flies towards his head that had shot out of Queen Isabo's index finger. "And HE had Merrick arrested for something HE did." Isabo spits coldly as two more icicles shoot out of her finger aiming for Prince Mortimer who ducks out of the way. "You had your brother arrested?" Queen Alora asks in disbelief before shivering. "Stop throwing icicles at my son and I'll consider letting Merrick go." King Marius offers harshly. Isabo drops her hand and grips the back of the chair in front of her as she leans towards King Marius. "Consider this; release Merrick or I will leave you in this icy fortress to fight your enemy alone." Queen Isabo counters angrily straightening her spine. "What do you mean 'fight my enemy alone'?" The King asks cautiously rising from his seat and holding up his hand to stop his son from speaking. "Merrick saw an army marching towards the Kingdom and they weren't wearing your crest. We rushed back here to warn you, but your guards arrested Merrick before he got the chance to say anything." Isabo explains crossly. King Marius does some quick thinking then turns to face his son, "Mortimer have scouts go out to confirm Queen Isabo's story." He orders harshly. "I will escort Queen Isabo down to the dungeons to see the prisoner." King Marius informs Queen Isabo darkly. "I- I-m c-com-ming w-with y-you," Queen Alora chatters firmly. The King gives a curt nod in agreement then strolls towards the door. He involuntarily shivers as he walks closer to his wife's end of the table. Queen Isabo ceases the use of her powers as a servant meets them at the door with fur coats in hand. Queen Isabo figures Queen Alora sent the servant to retrieve the furs while she was having words with the King. King Marius and Queen Alora bundle up then lead the way towards the Dungeon.

The King is surprised when they enter the dungeon and find the temperature considerably warmer. His jaw drops as he walks by a cell and sees a floating ball of fire warming the prisoners. Queen Isabo smiles as she sees the same fireball. *Merrick, you big softy*; Isabo thinks enchantingly. She runs past the King and Queen towards one of the guards. "Where did you take the man who was just brought in?" Queen Isabo asks sternly. "Straight back, last cell on the right." The guard says nervously. Isabo runs down the corrider calling out his name.

Merrick opens his eyes when he hears Isabo's sweet voice call his name. "Down here!" He hollers. Merrick hears footsteps running towards the cell then he sees a relieved looking Isabo and his heart instantly feels light. "Isabo." He breathes happily. She smiles at him. "Are you alright?" Isabo asks anxiously. Merrick nods, "I'm fine." He starts to say something else when she turns away from him and waves someone forward. Merrick hears more footsteps approaching then sees a guard with a set of keys. Merrick kills the fireball in his cell as the guard unlocks the door and Isabo runs into the cell and kneels before him. "They didn't hurt you did they?" She asks worriedly as she gives him a quick once over and brushes his hair out of his eyes tucking a lock of it behind his right ear.

Merrick shakes his head grinning. "I take it, you believe me?" he asks amusedly, his eyes dancing with delight. "Of course." Isabo responds simply with a shrug. Why?" He asks perplexed though overjoyed she does. "Because I know you." She states matter-of-factly as she holds out her hand and the guard places the keys in it. "Everything you told me and how proud your Father was when he told me about you, I knew you would never hurt anyone." Isabo explains further in a distracted voice as she focuses on unlocking Merrick's cuffs. The lock finally clicks and the metal bar springs open freeing Merrick's wrists. He pulls Isabo into a hug. "Thank you." He whispers endearingly filled with happiness. Isabo hugs him back. "You're welcome." She says contentedly then pulls back. "Now let's get you out of here!" Isabo recommends joyously as she stands up and helps Merrick to his feet.

Merrick keeps a hold of Isabo's hand as they turn towards the door. They halt their movement and Merrick's smile falters as he sees an older version of himself with short hair with grey streaks and brown eyes standing in the doorway. The man studies him intently. "You have the power of fire?" the man asks speculatively. "Yes Sir." Merrick replies nervously with a slight nod. "Why didn't you use your powers against the guards when they attacked you?" The man inquires gruffly. Merrick narrows his gaze at the man. "I'm not a monster. I would never intentionally hurt someone with or without my powers." Merrick answers darkly, offended by the question. He sees surprise flash in the man's eyes before his stoicism replaces it.

"Queen Isabo claims you saw an army marching this way. Is that true?" The King asks stonily. "Yes." Merrick growls; not liking the accusation of him or Isabo being a liar. "Do you know who they are?" The King asks in an aggravated tone. Merrick shakes his head. "I've never seen them before but this was on the flag one of the men was carrying." Merrick states flatly as he uses his free hand to create an image of a crest with two lions and a pair of crossed swords underneath them with fire. "Wallbren." The King mutters recognizing the crest immediately. The King turns away from Merrick and Isabo at the sound of someone approaching. "Your Majesty, the Wallbrenians are headed straight for us!" A scout reports anxiously and slightly out of breath as he stops a few feet away from the King. King Marius looks at the scout and gives a slight nod acknowledging that he understands.

"I should have known they would try a sneak attack." King Marius mutters darkly to no one in particular. "Get my General in arms." The King commands the scout gravely then he turns to the guard and points at Merrick. "This boy has been falsely accused. He is not an imposter. He is my son. Prince Mortimer was unaware he has a brother. Prince Merrick is free to go." King Marius states stoically. He then turns around without looking at Merrick and walks back up the corridor, grabbing Queen Alora's hand as he walks by her and pulls her along.

Merrick smirks at the guard. "I want my friend, Anton released." He states coolly as he points around Isabo to the gentleman sitting on the ground. The guard reluctantly walks over to Anton and releases him. "Thanks kid. I mean, your highness." Anton says appreciatively quickly correcting himself. Merrick waves off the title as he leads Isabo out of the cell with Anton right behind them. Merrick glances sideways at Isabo. "Do you think you can get rid of all this ice?" he asks teasingly his eyes twinkling with anticipation. "I can give it a whirl." She remarks dryly feigning nonchalance. Isabo winks at Merrick and smiles as she lets go of his hand. She raises her hands up and closes her eyes. Her hands glow a soft white as a flurry of snow swirls around them rapidly for a few minutes and then it's gone and so is all the ice.

"That is so cool!" Merrick exclaims ecstatically as he snaps his fingers and all the fire balls disappear. "Not bad yourself." Isabo comments approvingly then smiles at him. She grabs his hand and they regale their tales of what they did after Merrick was arrested as they walk up the hall while Anton follows them silently.

"Now what do we do?" Merrick asks lightly as they enter the main hall. "Well, I did promise the King I would try and help protect his Kingdom, so I guess I should go find him and see what he wants me to do." Queen Isabo remarks thoughtfully. "Then let's go find the King." Merrick spouts whimsically. "The King should be in the war room Prince Merrick." Anton pipes up uneasily. Merrick and Isabo turn to look at Anton. "Great, where's that?" Merrick asks innocently. "I shall lead you there." Anton replies graciously as he scurries around them. "If you will follow me your majesties." He requests obediently. "Lead the way." Isabo orders pleasantly. "And Anton, I'm no majesty. Just her. You can call me Merrick." He informs Anton casually as he spins Isabo forward making her laugh. Her laughter dies a moment later when they hear a voice yell, "You Fool!" They creep towards the room where the voice came from. The see a door partially open and creep up to it to listen in on the conversation.

"I told you to inform ME, and me alone, about the soldiers." Prince Mortimer snaps at the servant as he paces the study. "I'm sorry your highness, I could not find you." The scout explains fearfully. "Well, he only knows about the troops coming through the woods, they should reach the Blacksmith's in an hour. There haven't been any sightings of their ships yet, but they should be here in maybe two ..." Prince Mortimer contemplates to himself no longer paying any attention to the scout.

Merrick, Isabo and Anton quietly back away from the door and down another corridor. "I need to get to my Dad and Soot." Merrick whispers urgently as he turns, walking back the way they came. "Wait my Lord! I know a quicker way through a secret passage." Anton calls out in a hushed tone. Merrick turns back towards Anton. "Show me and its Merrick." Merrick states anxiously. Anton leads them down a small staircase to what looks like a small broom closet. He moves the rug on the floor revealing a trap door. Anton lifts it open. "Follow this all the way to the end and it leads out just inside the forest." Anton instructs rapidly. Merrick runs down the steps and then hears someone behind him. He looks over his shoulder and sees Isabo following him. "What are you doing? I thought you had to help the King?" He asks perplexedly as he walks quickly down the tunnel with a fireball in his hand to light the way. "I do, but I'm going to help you first." Queen Isabo replies diligently. Merrick holds out his free hand for her to take. "Thanks" he says gratefully; glad to have the company. She takes his hand and they break into a run.

When they come out of the secret passage, Merrick extinguishes his flame. He can tell they are about a half mile away from his home. Isabo and Merrick take a minute to catch their breath, before sprinting towards Merrick's place.

"Soot! Dad!" Merrick yells as soon as the shop comes in sight. Soot bounds towards Merrick and jumps on him knocking Merrick to the ground and licks his face. Merrick laughs, "It's good to see you too, Soot." He pants happily then gently pushes the wolf off him. "C'mon boy, we need to grab father and get out of here." Merrick states urgently as Isabo finally catches up to him. The three of them run into the fort and Merrick yells for his Dad again. His Father runs out of the house.

"Son what is … Why aren't you wearing your hood up?" His father asks worriedly. Merrick doesn't answer him; he just runs by him into the house. When Christian sees Queen Isabo standing a few feet away with Soot, he bows. "Queen Isabo what are you doing here?" Christian asks surprised to see her. "No time to explain, we need to leave." Queen Isabo informs him frantically walking briskly towards him as Merrick re-appears with a bag over his shoulder. "Let's go." He instructs quickly before running out of the fort with Isabo, Soot and his Father following his lead.

They are fortunate not to run into anyone on their way back to the entrance of the hidden passage. Once they are all safely in the secret tunnel, Isabo uses her powers to seal the entrance so no one else can use it. Then Merrick leads the way back.

Anton is awaiting them when Merrick emerges from the secret passage back into the storage room in the Castle. After everyone exits the tunnel and Anton closes the trap door, Queen Isabo seals that door shut with a layer of ice. Anton leads the four of them to the War room where the King, Prince Mortimer, and the General of Octavian's army are discussing strategy.

"We'll put archers on the northern and southern walls and have ground troops covering the east and west sides of the castle." The General dictates with authority. All three men look up from the map they're huddled around when Merrick, Isabo, and the others enter the room. The General's eyes widen in surprise when he focuses on Merrick for the first time.

"General, sir you can't do that. It risks too many peoples' lives." Merrick objects compellingly. "That's the cost of War." The General replies cavalierly. "It doesn't have to be." Merrick argues emphatically then looks to the King. "Please King Marius, let Queen Isabo use her gift to protect this Kingdom." Merrick pleads urgently. "What did you have in mind?" King Marius asks speculatively. "I can build a great wall around your kingdom to keep your enemies at bay." Isabo proposes rationally. The King stares at the map of his Kingdom as he thinks it over. After a few minutes, He looks up at the General, "General, station our men around the castle." He orders sharply then looks at Isabo. "Queen Isabo, do what you can to avoid unnecessary bloodshed." The King instructs firmly. Merrick smiles. "Thank you, your Highness" he breathes happily with relief; understanding an actual battle is the backup plan if Isabo's wall doesn't hold. Merrick turns towards Isabo to see her running out the door. He chases after her.

Merrick follows Isabo as she runs from one end of the castle to the other out onto the nearest balcony until she has built a 3 story wall clear around the kingdom. Queen Isabo and Merrick walk back to the North side balcony and wait for Wallbren's army to emerge. It's not long before they are joined by King Marius, Prince Mortimer, Anton, and Soot. King Marius stands parallel to Merrick, but with a good five feet of space between them. Soot lies down at Isabo's feet while Anton and Prince Mortimer mill around behind Merrick and Isabo.

Queen Isabo nudges Merrick in the ribs as she spots the first Wellbren soldiers emerge from the tree line. Merrick believes Isabo's wall is going to work because the soldiers are stopping as soon as they see the wall and appear baffled by it. "It's working." Merrick announces in excitement.

A moment later his joy vanquishes as he sees several men with axes run towards the wall and start hacking into it. Then more men appear out of the woods pulling a catapult behind them. The group on the balcony watches as the Wellbren soldiers flings a boulder engulfed in flames at the ice wall. It shatters through the top of the wall. Queen Isabo repairs the wall, but the Wellbrenian's bring out more catapults and it becomes too much for Isabo. "I'm not going to be able to hold them off much longer. They're destroying my wall faster than I can fix it." Isabo informs them distractedly with anxiety in her voice as she looks out at the grounds repairing the wall as quickly as she can.

She glances over at Merrick. "I'm sorry." She apologizes contritely. Merrick shakes his head at her. "Don't apologize. You're doing the best you can." He comforts her with a wan smile. He looks at King Marius. "You should warn the Kingdom to brace for attack." Merrick tells the King sadly; disappointed his idea didn't work. "Wait

Prince Merrick, you can save us." Anton pipes up nervously as he knows it is wrong to cut off the King when he had opened his mouth to say something. The King snaps his mouth shut and glares at his old advisor. "I told you it's just Merrick and how could I possibly save the Kingdom?" Merrick sighs in a despairing tone as he stares at the ground and runs a hand through his hair. "Your gift. Use your powers like the legend says. Create a wall of fire." Anton implores urgently. Merrick looks up at him in surprise. "I can't. I don't know how." Merrick confesses slightly hysterical. "Yes you can. I know you can." Isabo states sincerely.

Merrick spins around and looks at her. He sees the confidence she has in him. "All you have to do is close your eyes and picture it and your powers will do the rest." She tells him in a gentle voice with a warm smile and encouraging eyes. Merrick takes a deep breath and then faces the grounds. He closes his eyes and holds out his hands. Merrick imagines a great wall of fire surrounding the entire Kingdom and for the heat of the flame to expel out towards the forest and the sea. He feels his hands warm and then he hears gasps around him. Merrick opens his eyes and sees a great wall of fire where the ice wall had been.

"Now that's impressive." Queen Isabo states proudly with an impish grin. She goes to kiss Merrick on the cheek, but he turns his head to look at her just as she rises up on her tip toes leaning forward and she kisses him on the lips instead. Queen Isabo quickly breaks the kiss and blushes looking away from him. Merrick drops his hands turning them to normal color and beams at her. He wraps one arm around her shoulders. They marvel at his wall in silence until they hear someone calling out the King's name from behind them. They turn to see a soldier running towards them.

"King Marius the Wellbrenian's have surrendered!" The soldier exclaims excitedly as he huffs trying to catch his breath. "King Dorian of Wellbren requests to speak with you and the one who made the fire wall." The soldier pants. "Bring King Dorian here." King Marius instructs the soldier smugly. "How your Majesty? The wall of fire surrounds the entire Kingdom. There is no way to bring him through." The soldier replies; discombobulated by his King's orders. "The wall will be gone by the time you return to your post." King Marius informs him dismissively. The soldier gives a quick bow in understanding and runs back down the corridor. Merrick waits until the soldier is out of sight then snaps his fingers and the firewall vanishes instantly. "Show off." Isabo mutters teasingly as she kneels down to pet the sleeping Soot.

"May I present King Dorian of Wellbren." A servant announces a short time later. Merrick and Isabo look up from where they are sitting on the ground petting Soot. King Marius turns around and Prince Mortimer steps back out of the doorway. Merrick stands up and helps Isabo to her feet as the Wellbren King steps out onto the balcony. King Dorian glares at Prince Mortimer before directing his attention to King Marius. "I am here to inform your Majesty that your son, Mortimer, guaranteed us an easy victory and promised once we killed you he would surrender and agree to trade a quarter of your annual supply of coal for a quarter of our grains." King Dorian states coolly with a smirk as he sees the look of astonishment on the King's face. "And that is the only reason we attacked." King Dorian adds sternly; his smile vanishing.

"Is it true?" King Marius asks Mortimer in disbelief. Prince Mortimer straightens his spine and puffs out his chest. "Yes father, it is true" Prince Mortimer admits stoically. Why would you do such a thing?" King Marius asks incredulously; aghast by his son's attitude towards his admission. "I don't want to marry her." Prince Mortimer spits out defiantly pointing at Isabo. "I wasn't about to let you give

MY kingdom to him, so I came up with a plan to get rid of all three of you." Mortimer states in a despising tone; glaring at Merrick before turning his attention back to his father. "Guards, arrest Prince Mortimer." King Marius commands angrily to his men that had escorted King Dorian.

The guards advance on Mortimer, but he shoves them back and draws a knife. "This is entirely your fault!" Mortimer shouts angrily at Merrick as he runs at him with his knife raised. Isabo creates a patch of ice in front of Mortimer and he slips on it. Queen Isabo pulls Merrick back as Mortimer skids forward. Mortimer hits the edge of the balcony and topples over it. Merrick grabs Mortimer's leg before he plummets to the ground which would have ended in his death. Merrick pulls his brother up and back over the railing to safety then lets him go.

Mortimer pushes himself up on his hands and knees and the guards pull him to his feet. "Why did you save me?" Mortimer asks Merrick petulantly with a hint of shock. "Like I said before, I'm not a monster. I don't like seeing anyone get hurt." Merrick replies casually. "Take him to the dungeon." King Marius commands disgustedly. The guards drag Prince Mortimer away as he stares at Merrick in stunned silence.

"Are you the one who made the fire wall?" King Dorian asks curiously of Merrick. Merrick nods formally. "And what is your name?" King Dorian asks intrigued by Merrick as he looks him up and down. "He is my son, Prince Merrick." King Marius announces, jumping in before Merrick can say anything. "It's just Merrick." Merrick corrects the King annoyed by the fact that all of a sudden they think he needs a title when before today; No one in the Kingdom acknowledged his existence.

King Dorian smiles amusedly at Merrick's tenacity. "Well, I think you'll be a fine future King of Octavian." King Dorian states sincerely.

King Marius nods in agreement and says, "I agree. Now ..." "Whoa, wait. I don't want to be king." Merrick informs them; hastily cutting off King Marius's response. "WHAT!?" Both Kings exclaim in unison. "No offense, but I like being a blacksmith and I plan on returning to my home in the woods." Merrick states composedly. "But you're my son." King Marius utters in bafflement. "You're a Prince with a great gift. You shouldn't squander it as a Blacksmith." King Dorian interjects pointedly; aghast by the news. King Marius nods in agreement. "I may have been born a Prince, but I was raised by a Blacksmith and I'm not squandering my gift. I use it to build amazing things. It's what makes me happy. I've never been interested in living in a palace or to be a nobleman. I appreciate the offer, but I'm respectfully declining." Merrick explains patiently.

"Then who is going to take my place as King?" King Marius asks incredulously. "Mortimer." Merrick replies simply. "You expect me to let Mortimer rule after he tried to have me killed?" King Marius asks taken aback by the very notion. "Yeah. He wants to be King and your people love him. My Dad is always telling me what a great King Prince Mortimer will make because he takes the time to visit and understand his people; instead of, assuming he knows what's best for them. Just give him a few days in the dungeon to cool off and then make a truce with him." Merrick reasons casually. "Sounds fair" King Dorian agrees thoughtfully. King Marius lets out an exasperated sigh. "Very well" King Marius agrees, accepting Merrick's decision. "King Dorian, Queen Isabo If you'll follow me, we can finish negotiating both of your new treaties." King Marius states warily. King Dorian nods and follows King Marius out the door.

"I'll catch up to you gentleman in a moment." Queen Isabo calls out quickly. She turns to face Merrick and gives him a sad smile. "I guess this is goodbye if you're heading back to your home. I'll be returning to mine shortly after I sign the treaty with the King." She states forlornly. Merrick smiles, "Well, I was hoping you would let me come along with you. I'd like to see your Kingdom." He says warmly as he brushes a loose strand of hair out of her face. Queen Isabo blushes. "Only if you promise to bring Soot with you." She bargains impishly. "Deal." Merrick says happily then pulls Isabo into his arms and kisses her.

Merrick and Soot return to Arenia with Queen Isabo. Merrick enjoys her Kingdom so much he decides to stay. Merrick opens his own Blacksmith shop close to the Palace. He courts Queen Isabo and they eventually wed.

King Marius keeps Prince Mortimer imprisoned for three days. He then sits down with his youngest son and they have a long heart to heart talk and work out their differences. Prince Mortimer eventually takes his place as King. He maintains a good relationship between the Kingdoms of Arenia and Wellbren, bringing peace and prosperity throughout the lands.

The End

www.ingramcontent.com/pod-product-compliance
Lightning Source LLC
Chambersburg PA
CBHW072141150726
48002CB00004B/1577